# My Car by Byron Barton

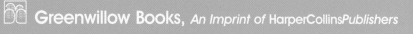
Greenwillow Books, *An Imprint of* HarperCollins*Publishers*

My Car. Copyright © 2001 by Byron Barton. Manufactured in China by South China Printing Company Ltd. All rights reserved. The full-color art was created in Adobe Photoshop™. The text type is Avant Garde Gothic. Library of Congress Cataloging-in-Publication Data: Barton, Byron. My car / written and illustrated by Byron Barton. p. cm. "Greenwillow Books." Summary: Sam describes in loving detail his car and how he drives it. ISBN 0-06-029624-0 (trade) — ISBN 0-06-029625-9 (lib. bdg.) — ISBN 0-06-058940-X (pbk.) [1. Automobiles—Fiction.] I. Title. PZ7.B2848 My 2001 [E]—dc21 00-050334 For information address HarperCollins Children's Books, a division of HarperCollins Publishers, 10 East 53rd Street, New York, NY 10022. First Edition 13 SCP 20 19 18 17 16 15

I
am
Sam.

This
is
my
car.

I
love
my
car.

I keep
my
car
clean.

My
car
needs
oil

# and a full tank

of gasoline.

# My car has many parts.

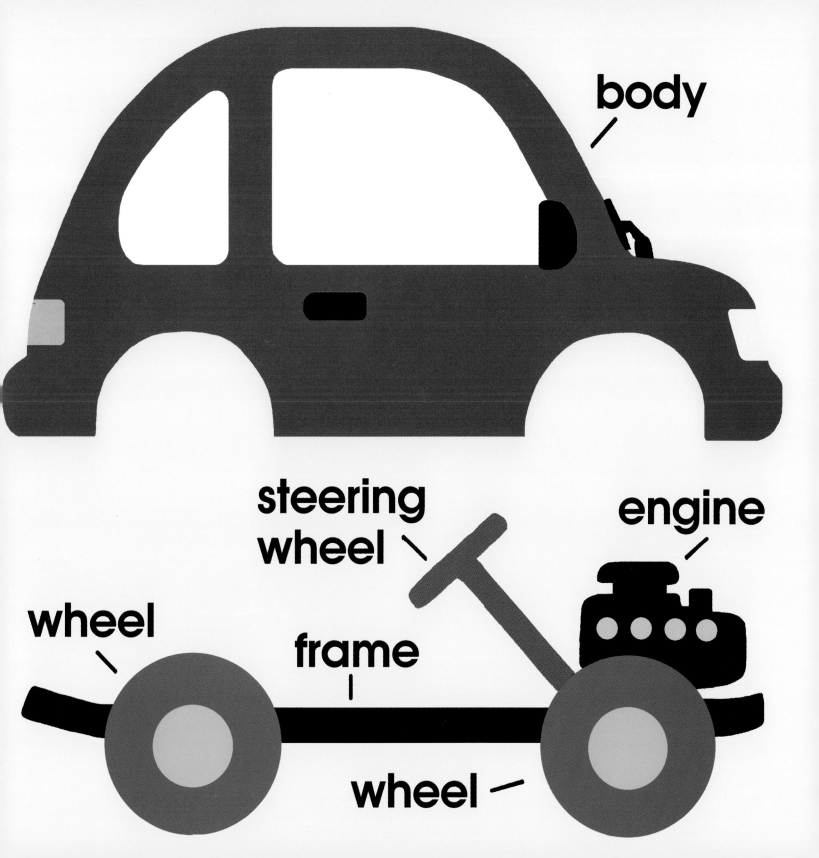

body

steering
wheel

engine

wheel

frame

wheel

My car has lights to see at night

# and windshield wipers

to see in the rain.

# When I drive,

# I drive carefully.

I obey

# the laws.

I stop

# for pedestrians.

BUS

MAIN ST

ONE WAY

NO PARKING

I read the signs.

I
drive
my
car
to
many
places.

# I drive my car to work.

# I drive

my bus.

beep beep